Quite the Same

Annette Darity Garber
Illustrated by Allison Rich

Acknowledgements

A huge thank you to my talented husband, Jarred Garber, who walked with me through the various stages of putting this book into print. His attention to detail, savvy planning and knowledge of the process were huge gifts to me!

Thank you also to our daughter, Jaida Garber, who created the seven sketches, etched in the margins of "the letter" that traveled around the world in this book.

I am so grateful to my longtime friend, Claudia Good, who inspired me through her own brave endeavors and encouraging words, to keep this dream alive.

And finally, I am eternally grateful to Allison Rich for her generosity of time, illustrative talent and enthusiasm for this project.

Text © 2016 by Annette Garber
Illustrations © 2016 by Allison Rich

Published by Annette Garber, 2016
Printed by Brilliant Graphics, Inc., Exton, PA

ISBN: 978-0-692-73712-5

Dedication

To Dylan and Jaida, who have taught me
how beautiful and sensitive
and strong the spirit of a child is.
A.G.

To the Westerners, Easterners,
Cowboys, Mennonites, and Chicagoans
that make up my beautiful family.
A.R.

I'm Emma from America
and I just turned eleven.

I've been sitting in a
wheelchair since
I was only seven.

There was an
accident, you see.
And I haven't been
the same.

I cannot walk
or run or splash
in puddles
when it rains.

I used to love to swim,
do gymnastics and ballet.

I got dressed
all by myself,
walked to the park
on sunny days.

Sometimes, when I am bored,
I feel sorry for myself.
But today, while in my bedroom,
I found this note upon my shelf.

I do not know your name
or the color of your eyes.
I wonder what makes you laugh.
I wonder what makes you cry.
Maybe you are tall or short,
black or white or brown.
Do you live in a big city
    or in a little town?
All I really want to say
Is that I care, it's true.
That sometimes I feel lonely
    and sad and angry, too.
And if I lived beside you
    I'd come to know your name.
You'd be my friend and I'd be yours;
    we're really quite the same.
So close your eyes, cause here's a hug:
    it's sent from me to you.
And share this with another
    who's sad and lonely, too.

希望

My name is Pedro.
I am eight. I live in Mexico.

I play soccer, go to school,
and have a best amigo.

Today is very sad,
and I do not want to play.
My papi couldn't find a job
and had to go away.

We don't know
when we'll see him;
it could be two whole years.
Christmas without Papi
will be Christmas
shedding tears.

The strangest thing just happened.
Something just fell from the skies.
I opened this paper airplane and
read through blurry eyes:

I do not know your name
or the color of your eyes.
I wonder what makes you laugh.
I wonder what makes you cry,
Maybe you are tall or short,
black or white or brown.
Do you live in a big city
or in a little town?
All I really want to say
Is that I care, it's true.
That sometimes I feel lonely
and sad and angry, too.
And if I lived beside you
I'd come to know your name.
You'd be my friend and I'd be yours;
we're really quite the same.
So close your eyes, cause here's a hug;
it's sent from me to you.
And share this with another
who's sad and lonely, too.

希望

I am Kirsten who usually smiles
but today is feeling sad.

I went to my new school today
and my new friends made me mad.

One boy pointed at
my freckles;
another laughed at
my red curls.

And when it was
time for recess,
I was teased by
all the girls.

I wander to the ocean,
let the water tickle my toes.
I wonder if I'll find a friend
who doesn't mind my freckled nose.

Just now I see a bottle
bopping in the green sea waves.
I reach for it, pop the cork,
and read what the water gave:

I do not know your name
or the color of your eyes.
I wonder what makes you laugh.
I wonder what makes you cry.
Maybe you are tall or short,
black or white or brown.
Do you live in a big city
or in a little town?
All I really want to say
Is that I care, it's true.
That sometimes I feel lonely
and sad and angry, too.
And if I lived beside you
I'd come to know your name.
You'd be my friend and I'd be yours;
we're really quite the same.
So close your eyes, cause here's a hug:
it's sent from me to you.
And share this with another
who's sad and lonely, too.

希望

I'm Luka from Russia
and turning ten today.

But in my orphanage
We don't celebrate birthdays.

Even so, every year...
I pray the same old,
simple prayer:
I wish for a mother and father,
a family who wants me near.

I cannot help but cry
when I know deep
down, it's true.
When I wake up tomorrow
morning, I'll still be cold,
alone and blue.

While the wind wipes these tears,
it blows a letter through the air.
I reach for it, open it,
and read the message there:

I do not know your name
or the color of your eyes.
I wonder what makes you laugh.
I wonder what makes you cry.
Maybe you are tall or short,
black or white or brown.
Do you live in a big city
or in a little town?
All I really want to say
Is that I care, it's true
That sometimes I feel lonely
and sad and angry, too.
And if I lived beside you
I'd come to know your name.
You'd be my friend and I'd be yours;
we're really quite the same.
So close your eyes, cause here's a hug;
it's sent from me to you.
And share this with another
who's sad and lonely, too.

希望

RUSSIA

Enaya is my name
and I'm from Palestine.

I've been wishing for world peace,
where everyone is kind.

I've grown up in a land
with barriers and walls.
Why is there so much fighting?
Why can't we get along?

Muslim, Jewish, Christian...
It shouldn't matter how we're named.
Arab or Israeli, we are mostly quite the same.

Just now as I was dreaming,
a peace dove visited my home.
She brought this little letter
to say I'm not alone:

My name is Moses
        and I come from South Sudan.

My family lives
in Kenya now;
we had to leave our
beautiful land.

You see, there were
some soldiers who came
to destroy our home.

We walked many
days to get here;
safety is why
we roamed.

I try not to complain,
but life is hard here in the tents.
A lot of sickness, not much food,
I try to be content.

Just today when I
was mad that there
was no more bread,
this little plane fell to the ground
and this is what it said:

I do not know your name
or the color of your eyes.
I wonder what makes you laugh.
I wonder what makes you cry.
Maybe you are tall or short,
black or white or brown.
Do you live in a big city
or in a little town?
All I really want to say
Is that I care, it's true.
That sometimes I feel lonely
and sad and angry, too.
And if I lived beside you
I'd come to know your name.
You'd be my friend and I'd be yours;
we're really quite the same.
So close your eyes, cause here's a hug:
it's sent from me to you.
And share this with another
who's sad and lonely, too.

KENYA

My name is Asako
  and I live in Japan.

What I'd like to be when I grow up
is a doctor if I can.

My brother,
he is very smart.
He only brings home A's.
But for me, school
is very hard.
I feel stupid on most days.

And even though
I stayed up late
to study for my test,
I failed again, you see,
and, yes, I tried my best.

But just when I was feeling dumb
and not so very smart,
this paper boat came sailing to me.
It poured hope into my heart:

I do not know your name
or the color of your eyes.
I wonder what makes you laugh.
I wonder what makes you cry.
Maybe you are tall or short,
black or white or brown.
Do you live in a big city
        or in a little town?
All I really want to say
Is that I care, it's true.
That sometimes I feel lonely
    and sad and angry, too.
And if I lived beside you
    I'd come to know your name.
You'd be my friend and I'd be yours;
    we're really quite the same.
So close your eyes, cause here's a hug:
    it's sent from me to you.
And share this with another
who's sad and lonely, too.

希望

Resources

Resources for Teachers

TeachUNICEF provides educators with global learning resources and programs focusing upon global citizenship and children's rights.
www.TeachUNICEF.org

The Global Dimension is a website to support teachers in bringing a global dimension to their classrooms by providing various resources for all age groups.
https://GlobalDimension.org.uk

The International Education and Resource Network (iEARN) is a non-profit educational network that connects schools and youth organizations around the globe, empowering young people to work collaboratively in finding solutions to real world issues.
us.iEARN.org

Take Action

Letter to a Friend

Do you have a friend who might be feeling sad or lonely? Who can you think of who would love to receive a letter or a hand-drawn picture in the mail? Bring a smile to your friend's face by sending him or her something that you created!

Letter to a Child in the Hospital

Did you know that you can send letters to other friends you haven't even met? Children that are really "quite the same" as you are and who are in the hospital right now? Bring a smile to a new friend's face by letting him or her know you care.
Visit www.CardsForHospitalizedKids.com to learn more!

Letter to a Representative

Did you know that you can write letters online to your local representatives that work at the White House? You can ask them to help pass laws that keep children safe and care for children who are hurting.
Visit www.IJM.org/get-involved/advocacy to learn how!